I Dreamed I Was A Big Baboon

By Debra A. Johnson

Illustrated
by
Stephanie Kranz

Published by Abdo & Daughters, 4940 Viking Drive, Suite 622, Edina, Minnesota 55435.

Library bound edition distributed by Rockbottom Books, Pentagon Tower, P.O. Box 36036, Minneapolis, Minnesota 55435.

Printed in the United States.

All Illustrations: Stephanie Kranz

Edited by Julie Berg

LIBRARY OF CONGRESS CATALOGING-IN-PUBLICATION DATA

Johnson, Debra, A., 1961—
     I Dreamed I was-- A Big Baboon / Debra A. Johnson.
         p.   cm. -- (I Dreamed I was--)
Summary: A child dreams of being a baboon and meeting some of the other animals in Africa.
ISBN 1-56239-305-7
[1. Animals--Fiction. 2. Baboons--Fiction. 3. Dreams--Fiction.
4. Africa--Fiction. 5.Stories in Rhyme.]   I. Title.   II. Title: Big Baboon.
III. Series: Johnson, Debra A., 1961- I Dreamed I was--
PZ8.3.J6317Iad   1994
[E]--dc20   94-17410
                                                  CIP
                                                  AC

I Dreamed I Was A Big Baboon

Debra A. Johnson

I was in my bedroom playing
and it was such a mess.
Clothes and toys were scattered
from the doorway to the desk.

As I put away my things
to make my bedroom clean,
my imagination led me
through the most fantastic dream.

I dreamed I was a big baboon
chewing on a leaf.
Many other monkeys appeared
in colors beyond belief.

I was in the jungles of Africa
when I witnessed something strange.
As a chameleon went from leaf to leaf
I saw its colors change.

Then I met a tall giraffe
whose neck was eight feet long.
It was browsing around the countryside
and asked me to come along.

We saw herds of antelope—
nearly 25 different breeds.
Like the dik-dik and the eland
and the white-bearded wildebeest.

The leopard and the cheetah
look quite a bit the same.
But leopards have bigger heads
and the cheetah's neck has a mane.

The lion's the king of the forest.
That's a bubble I don't want to burst.
Though the queen is the one that goes hunting,
the king is the one that eats first.

The rhinoceros loves to take mud baths
to protect its skin from flies.
On its nose it has two horns
that must get in the way of its eyes.

The warthog appears to be hairless
but, in fact, it has a long narrow mane.
The wart-like things on its face
are what gives this wild pig its name.

**When a hippopotamus is swimming
it is very hard to spot it.
Its eyes and ears and nostrils
are all that stick out of the water.**

The elephant is mighty and strong.
Its trunk does much more than smell.
It is used to get water for drinking,
but can lift a huge log as well.

The zebra's a beautiful animal
whose stripes show up clearly by day.
But at night when the sun begins setting
it blends in with the grass and looks gray.

My time with the giraffe was over
and I bid farewell to my friends.
I can't wait to fall asleep tonight
so I can dream again!

GLOSSARY

Antelope - an animal found on the plains of western North America.

Chameleon - a small lizard that can change the color of its skin to blend in with its surroundings.

Cheetah - a large cat with spots that is found in Asia and Africa.

Hippopotamus - a huge, thick-skinned, almost hairless animal found in or near the rivers of Africa.

Leopard - a large cat of Africa and Asia, having a yellowish fur spotted with black.

Rhinoceros - a thick-skinned animal of Africa and Asia with one or two upright horns on its snout.

Sable - a flesh-eating animal somewhat like a weasel, but larger.

Warthog - a pig-like animal of Africa with warts on its face.

Wildebeest - a large moose-like animal of Africa.